Build a
Birdhouse

adapted by Natalie Shaw
based on the screenplay "Home Tweet Home"
written by Betty Quan

Ready-to-Read

Simon Spotlight
New York London Toronto Sydney New Delhi

SIMON SPOTLIGHT
An imprint of Simon & Schuster Children's Publishing Division
1230 Avenue of the Americas, New York, New York 10020
This Simon Spotlight edition January 2020
© 2020 The Jim Henson Company. JIM HENSON'S mark & logo, DOOZERS mark & logo,
characters and elements are trademarks of The Jim Henson Company. All Rights Reserved.
All rights reserved, including the right of reproduction in whole or in part in any form.
SIMON SPOTLIGHT, READY-TO-READ, and colophon are registered trademarks of
Simon & Schuster, Inc.
For information about special discounts for bulk purchases, please contact Simon & Schuster
Special Sales at 1-866-506-1949 or business@simonandschuster.com.
Manufactured in the United States of America 1119 LAK
10 9 8 7 6 5 4 3 2 1
ISBN 978-1-5344-4551-2 (pb)
ISBN 978-1-5344-4552-9 (hc)
ISBN 978-1-5344-4553-6 (eBook)

It is morning in
Doozer Creek.

Molly Bolt wakes up
and goes downstairs.

There is a bird

in her house!

"Do you think it wants to

live here?"

Molly Bolt asks her parents.

"I sure hope not,"

says her mom.

Molly Bolt asks the Pod Squad for help!

When they arrive,

Flex shouts,

"There is a bird in your house!"

Daisy Wheel wants the bird
to live at her house instead.

"That bird needs its

own house,"

Spike says.

"Maybe we can build

a perfect home for it!"

Molly Bolt says.

Molly Bolt wants the home
to have a bathtub.

Daisy Wheel wants a window on the roof.

Flex wants a slide!

They get the bathtub,

window, and slide.

They go to the tree where

Molly Bolt lives.

They build the home

on the ground by the tree.

"It is perfect!"

says Flex.

The bird tries out the

new home.

The bird does not like it!

It flies back up to

the Bolt house.

Professor Gimbal explains that birds and Doozers like different things.

The Pod Squad built a home

for a Doozer instead of a bird!

To find out what a bird needs,

they go to look at a nest.

They make a plan for a home that is small and cozy like the nest.

They build the home and
use a crane to lift it.

They place it up high

in the tree!

The bird loves it
and moves in!

"There is nothing to it

when you do, do, do it!"

the Pod Squad cheers.